Black Boy, Black Boy

written by Crown Shepherd & illustrated by Mychal Batson

Black Boy, Black Boy

written by Crown Shepherd & illustrated by Mychal Batson

Edited by Lily Coyle
Illustrated by Mychal Batson
Production editor: Hanna Kjeldbjerg

ISBN 13: 978-1-64343-881-8
Library of Congress Catalog Number: 2019917579
Printed in the United States of America
First Printing: 2020
24 23 22 21 20   5 4 3 2 1

Book design and typesetting by Mychal Batson.

Beaver's Pond Press
939 Seventh Street West
Saint Paul, MN 55102
(952) 829-8818
www.BeaversPondPress.com

To order, visit www.crownthewriter.com. Reseller discounts available.

Contact Crown Shepherd at www.crownthewriter.com for school visits, speaking engagements, freelance writing projects, and interviews.

For all the Black Boys out there dreaming.
—CS

Be creative. Be fearless. Dream **BIG**.
—MB

Black Boy,
Black Boy,

what do you see?

I see a beautiful strong black man looking at me.

I am him.
He is me.

Black Boy,
Black Boy,

what do you see?

I see a doctor looking at me.

He likes to help people,
just like me.

Black Boy,
Black Boy,

what do you see?

I see a judge looking at me.

He is fair,
just like me.

Black Boy,
Black Boy,

what do you see?

Black Boy,
Black Boy,

what do you see?

Black Boy,
Black Boy,

what do you see?

I see a president looking at me.

He is powerful, just like me.

Black Boy,
Black Boy,

what do you see?

I see an artist looking at me.

He's creative, just like me.

I see an astronaut
looking at me.

He's amongst
the stars,
just like me.

Black Boy,
Black Boy,

what do you see?

I see an engineer looking at me.

He's building a robot, just like me.

Black Boy,
Black Boy,

what do you see?

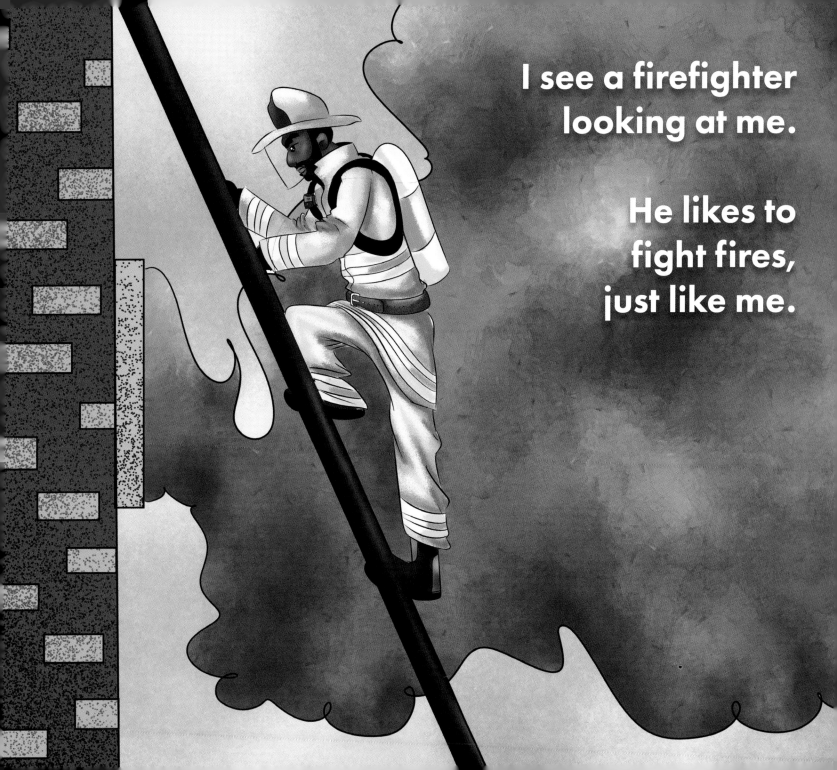

I see a firefighter looking at me.

He likes to fight fires, just like me.

Black Boys, Black Boys, what do you see?

Crown Shepherd is an emerging fiction, picture book, and comic book writer. Her writing is a result of her surroundings and upbringing. She has always been deeply rooted in literature and writing, but it wasn't until she found more writers that look like her that her writing soared. Those writers allowed her to dream and create by her own standards, and from a point of view of a Black protagonist. As someone from an underrepresented community, Crown knows what it means to have representation feed your creativity. The stories she wants to share are aimed at giving a voice to the voiceless.

Mychal Batson is a multidisciplinary artist and entrepreneur from St. Paul, Minnesota who's scribbled on pages and drawn in margins since he was old enough to hold a pencil. After graduating from Augsburg College with a degree in creative writing, he taught himself design and illustration.

Mychal believes Black art and education is incredibly important, and that inspiring future artists and dreamers to create entirely new worlds using their imagination is a revolutionary act.

"If you can read, you can learn!
If you can learn, you can grow!
And if you can grow, you can be anything!"
—Crown Shepherd